The oil painting on the inside cover, entitled, "ROSE AND HER FOAL" was done by Jane Davidian. For more information about Jane, go to www.janedavidian.com.

This book is lovingly dedicated to my dear sons, JT and Jesse, whom I love and teach every day.

I want to thank Uncle J who spent countless hours helping me make one of my dreams come true. I also want to thank Nana and the rest of my family for their loyalty and support.

ISBN: 1-4196-3465-8
ISBN-13: 978-1419634659

Rose's Foal

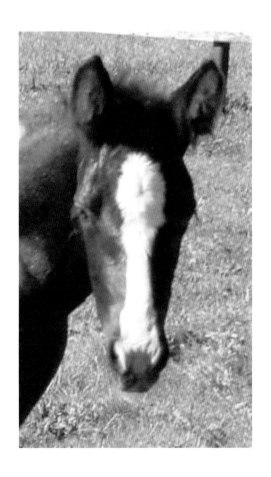

Story and Pictures
By
Scarlett Lewis

This is Rose. Rose lives on Wild Rose Farm in Connecticut. She is a Percheron draft horse. Rose's color is dapple gray.

Draft horses are the tallest, heaviest, and strongest breed of horse. They are used to pull carriages and to do farm work. They also have the gentlest nature of any breed.

Rose pulls a plow on the farm, but she is not working now. She is going to have a baby soon. A baby horse is called a "foal."

Rose is hungry because she is eating not only for herself; but also for the foal inside her. Her tummy is big and round because the foal is growing and preparing to meet the new world!

Rose knows that having a foal will be a lot of responsibility. She also knows that it will be lots of fun. Rose and the foal will be good company for each other. They will love each other very much.

One morning, just as the sun's rays peek through the barn, and before the birds begin to sing, the foal is born!

The foal is a boy, so he is called a "colt." The colt is snowy white with black spots. He has the markings of an Indian pony, so his mother names him Little Chief. Little Chief is tired after being born and takes a nap while his mother quietly munches hay close by.

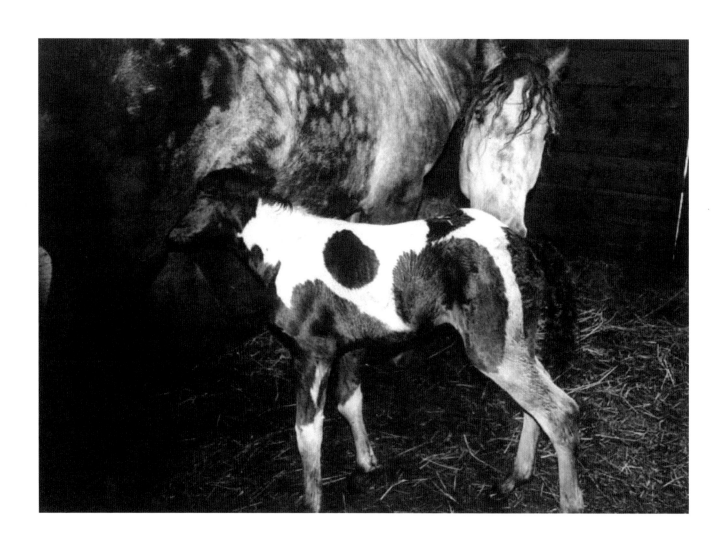

When Little Chief wakes up, he is hungry. He drinks milk from his mother, and his belly grows full. He feels warm and secure with his mother in the safety of their stall.

In the beginning, Little Chief sleeps most of the time. He needs rest because he is growing. His mother stands close by to watch over him.

The colt is very wobbly on his legs at first, but he quickly learns to balance. He is able to go outside and run with his mother after only one day! When horses live in the wild, they must be able to run with the herd as quickly as possible, to escape danger.

Someone is already waiting to meet Little Chief when the barn door is opened. It is a friendly dog who lives on the farm. The colt has never seen a dog before. They introduce themselves by touching noses, as some animals do.

Then mother and son head out to the big pasture. It is a beautiful day, the sun is shining, and the air is crisp and inviting.

As they walk outside the paddock together, Rose gives her son important advice. She says, "It's a wonderful world out here. Keep your eyes and heart open. Try to look for the good in everything and find joy in all that surrounds you. Remember to be thankful for your blessings."

At first, Little Chief stays very close to his mother. The world seems so big, and he feels so small in it!

After several days pass, Little Chief becomes more adventurous. "Come on, Mom, let's go explore!"

Rose and Little Chief run around the big pasture, looking at the birds and the trees, happy to be together.

The colt takes many naps: playing and growing take a lot of energy! His mother always watches over him while he sleeps.

In a month, the colt is bigger, and can eat grass like his mother. He likes the fresh green taste, but he still likes his mother's milk best.

Rose teaches Little Chief everything she knows, even how to swish his tail to keep the pesky flies away.

The colt learns how to wear a halter like his mother. Someday he will wear a saddle and take people for rides around the pasture. He might also learn to pull a carriage or a plow. Little Chief likes learning new things.

Rose instructs Little Chief to always put his best hoof forward. She teaches him that it takes strength to be kind and gentle. She also tells him to put himself in someone else's horseshoes to understand how they feel.

Rose explains to her son that sometimes you have to be brave to be truthful. Little Chief listens to everything his mother says and promises he will try his best. This makes his mother very happy.

Rose also tells her son that one day they might not live on the same farm, but she will always love him. She explains that every mother and child share a special bond in their hearts, regardless of distance or time, forever and always.

Love Never Ends.

Scarlett Lewis lives with her family on Wild Rose Farm in Connecticut. She has been involved in all aspects of equine affairs, including showing, racing, and breeding. Besides managing her farm, Scarlett works in education, finance and real estate. She breeds Spanish Norman horses and is an avid gardener, artist and mother.

Rose lives on the farm with her son, Chief Crazy Horse, who was born on September 10, 2001.

www.wildrosefarm.net

19680728R00020

Made in the USA
Lexington, KY
02 January 2013